Bear's Dream

No part of this publication may be reproduced, or stored in a retrieval system, or transmitted in any form or by any means, electronic, mechanical, photocopying, recording, or otherwise, without written permission of the publisher. For information regarding permission, write to Scholastic Inc., Attention: Permissions Department, 555 Broadway, New York, NY 10012.

ISBN: 0-439-19096-7

Copyright © 1999 Tucker Slingsby Ltd. All rights reserved. Published by Scholastic Inc. SCHOLASTIC, CARTWHEEL BOOKS and associated logos are trademarks and/or registered trademarks of Scholastic Inc.

Library of Congress Cataloging-in-Publication Data available

10 9 8 7 6 5 4 3 2

00 01 02 03 04

Printed in the U.S.A. First American edition, October 2000

Bear's Dream

by Janet Slingsby
Illustrated by Tony Morris

SCHOLASTIC INC.

New York   Toronto   London   Auckland   Sydney
Mexico City   New Delhi   Hong Kong

Cartwheel BOOKS®

One wintry night, Teddy Bear couldn't get to sleep. "Humph," he said crossly and sat up in bed.

By the window, a large book lay open on the floor. He slid out of bed and went over to take a look. The book was full of photographs of real bears. There were bears fishing in a river and bears playing in the snow.

How wonderful to be a wild bear! thought Teddy Bear. *I'd like to run wild and have adventures. I'm bored with being a teddy bear.*

As he thought about running away and what he would need to pack in his backpack — a clean handkerchief and his eyeglasses — his eyelids began to droop lower and lower . . .

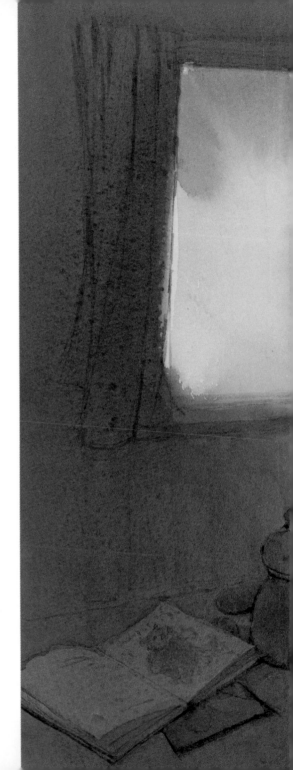

Splash! A shower of cold water hit Teddy Bear in the face.
"What was that?" he cried.

Whoosh! More cold water trickled down his fur. He opened his
eyes and saw two brown bear cubs standing on a riverbank.

"What kind of wild bears are you?" asked Teddy Bear.
"And why are you so wet?"

"We are grizzly bears," said one of the cubs.
"We've been helping our mother catch fish.
Come and try."

"This is my first adventure," said Teddy Bear bravely.

The mother bear, who was very, very big, stood in the rushing water. She held a huge, silvery fish in her paws.
   "Would you like to catch some salmon?" cried the cubs.

Teddy Bear thought about the cold water. He thought about eating raw, slippery fish . . . and shuddered.

He waved good-bye to the grizzly bear cubs and trotted away.

"**Mmmm,**" Teddy Bear said, feeling the hot sun on his damp fur.

"This looks like the right place to have a dry, warm sort of adventure!"

He stared at the dry grass and the tall trees. In the distance, he saw a herd of animals hopping by.

"Real kangaroos!" he cried.

As he watched the kangaroos, the sun beat down.

This adventure is getting a bit too warm, Teddy Bear thought. *I wish I had a cold drink.*

And he sat down in the shade of a big tree.

Teddy Bear heard a noise
and looked up into the tree.
He saw something and climbed
the tree to see what it was.

"What kind of wild bear are you?"
he asked the sleepy creature.

"I'm not a bear, I'm a koala," yawned the creature. "You woke me up. I usually sleep all day and have a nice dinner at night."

"What do you eat?" asked Teddy Bear, who was feeling hungry now as well as thirsty.

"Leaves, delicious leaves," said the koala. "Try one."

"Ugh," choked Teddy Bear. "I don't think I like these leaves. May I have a drink, please?"

"Oh, I don't drink water," said the koala. "I only eat leaves. The leaves give me water."

"This new adventure is not much fun!" said Teddy Bear. "I am hot, hungry, *and* thirsty."

So he waved good-bye to the koala and trotted away, wishing he had packed some sandwiches and a drink.

Just then, Teddy Bear heard a loud slurping, sucking, snuffling sort of sound. He hurried off to look and found a strange bear with his nose in a hole in the ground.

"What kind of wild bear are you?" asked Teddy Bear.
  "I am a sloth bear," said the bear, pulling his nose out of the hole.
    "What are you doing?" asked Teddy Bear.
    "I'm sucking up ants and termites," said the sloth bear.
    "Why?" asked Teddy Bear, amazed.
    "To eat them, of course," replied the sloth bear.

As Teddy Bear had no desire to eat ants and termites, he quickly waved good-bye to the sloth bear and trotted away.

"I thought wild bears ate honey," said Teddy Bear sadly.

"*I* eat honey," said a growly voice. "It's my favorite food."

"What kind of wild bear are you?" asked Teddy Bear.

"I am a sun bear," said the big bear. "If you want some honey, climb on my back and hold on tight!"

This adventure is *a little scary,* thought Teddy Bear bravely, as he clambered onto the sun bear's back.

The sun bear began to climb a very tall tree. As he climbed higher and higher, Teddy Bear shut his eyes.

But he opened them again when he heard the sound of angry buzzing. The sun bear had his paw inside a bees' nest and angry bees were flying all around them!

One large bee stung Teddy Bear on the nose. "Ouch," he cried, and he let go. Next thing he knew, he was falling down . . .

"As far as I am concerned," said
Teddy Bear, "honey should come in jars."
  He was hanging in a big green bush,
his backpack hooked over a branch.
He rubbed his sore nose.

"What's honey?" said a soft voice next to him.

"I know what kind of wild bear you are," said Teddy Bear. "You are a panda."

"You're right," said the baby panda, "but I am not a bear."

"What kind of food do you eat?" asked Teddy Bear, who thought pandas looked a lot like bears but was too hungry to argue. He hoped pandas ate cake and sandwiches.

"Come and meet my mom," said the baby panda. "She will give you some bamboo."

Teddy Bear was very disappointed to discover that bamboo was a green stick. One shoot was quite enough!

"I'm afraid I can't stay," said Teddy Bear. "I have to go off in search of more adventures."

He waved good-bye and trotted away.

It looks like that bear is wearing glasses, thought
Teddy Bear. "What kind of wild bear are you?"
he asked.

"I am a spectacled bear," said the strange-looking bear.
"My fur makes me look as if I am wearing glasses."

The spectacled bear was sitting in a tree, eating fruit.
He gave some to Teddy Bear. It was the best wild bear
food Teddy Bear had tried.

"I like it here," said Teddy Bear, looking at the mountains
in the distance. "Perhaps I can live like a wild spectacled
bear for a few days." And he began to search in his
backpack for his glasses.

Suddenly Teddy Bear heard loud shouts. A big clod of dirt flew past, just missing his sore nose. "What's happening?" he cried.

"It's the villagers," shouted the spectacled bear. "Run away as fast as you can!" And the spectacled bear rushed away without stopping to say good-bye.

Teddy Bear trotted after him as fast as he could, his backpack bobbing up and down on his back.

"Now where am I?" said
Teddy Bear. "It's so cold and there's
nothing but snow and ice here. No
bears at all. What shall I do?"

Then he saw big paw prints in the
snow. "Perhaps they'll lead me to a
bear. This is a very cold adventure,"
said Teddy Bear with a shiver. "I wish
I had packed a sweater."

Then Teddy Bear saw a black dot in
the distance. He trotted toward it.
As he got closer, he saw that the black
dot was the nose of a huge white bear.

"What kind of wild bear are you?" he
asked, feeling a little scared.
   "I'm a polar bear," she said. "Come
and meet my cubs."

Two polar bear cubs
were playing in the snow.
  "Come and slide on the ice
with us," they cried.

Teddy Bear played in the
snow until he was soaked to
his stuffing. He was very glad
when Mother Bear said it was
time to go home. He was
looking forward to drying
out in front of a warm fire.

The polar bears

disappeared down a hole in the snow. Teddy Bear scurried after them.

"Is this where you live?" he asked, a little disappointed. The polar bears' den had no fire and no furniture. It was just a hole in the ice.

Teddy Bear curled up between the sleeping cubs and tried not to think about his cozy bed at home. "This is an adventure!" he said in a small voice. His eyelids began to droop lower and lower . . .

When Teddy Bear woke up, he was lying on his bedroom floor at home.

"There you are!" a voice said. A little hand came down and pulled him back into bed. "Where have you been?"
   I've been dreaming about lots of adventures, thought Teddy Bear, snuggling down happily into the warm, cozy bed.

Then he looked down at his backpack and saw a bamboo shoot caught in the strap.